ERIC'S PARENTS DIVORCED

Candice Bell

ISBN-13: 9798831443400
ISBN-10: 1477123456

Cover design by: Art Painter
Library of Congress Control Number: 2018675309
Printed in the United States of America

*Always remember you can not control other people
you just have to be the best version of you.*

The tears rolled down Eric's face as he watched his father leave the home. Eric's mom and dad divorced and now dad was moving out. Eric, his brother, and sisters did not understand why mommy and daddy were mad at each other. Everything seemed like it was okay, mommy and daddy was not arguing with each other. He thought his parents were happy.

Before Eric's dad left, he told him it was not his fault and things would be the same. Eric could not help but feel like he was to blame, he closed the door behind his dad and ran to his room. He slammed the door and cried like a baby. He punched his pillow and threw his things around the room. "What did we do to daddy"? Eric thought.

He tried to lay down but could not sleep he punched a hole in his closet door, he knew he would get in trouble but didn't care. Eric did not want to live in the house anymore, he wanted to move with dad across town. "Why would he leave me?" he mumbled to himself. Then Eric sat on the bed, his tears rolled down some more.

After a few moments of crying, Eric wiped his face and came storming out of his room. He rushed down the hallway yelling and swinging his arms wildly. Eric's younger brother Emir, who also was in the hallway at the time, got hit in the face by Eric's arm and began crying. Emir ran to their mom's room and told her what happened. "Mom" with tears in his eyes "Eric hit me."

Eric's mom called for him and told him he was in time out for hitting and could not play his game or use his cell phone.Eric was so mad he went back to his room and threw his controller across his room floor. He continued his tantrum by snatching his clothes off the hangers in the closet and throwing them on the floor. He lay down in his bed refusing to eat dinner and went to bed early ready for the day to be over.

Eric slept the entire night, and the next morning was woken up by his mom for school. Eric woke up still upset from yesterday he quickly took a bath brushed his teeth and got ready for school, he did not speak to his mom or siblings. Eric's mom told him she knew he was upset but wanted him to focus on school and that he was loved very much. Eric said "okay," hugged his mom like he always did and left to walk to the bus stop with his sisters and brother.

Once at the bus stop Eric makes fun of a little kid's shoes and the kid began to cry. Eric and his friends laugh as Eric dances with joy. The bus pulls up and all the kids get on the bus, as they are walking up the steps, Eric pushes another kid, and he almost falls.

The Bus driver grabs Eric by his arm calmly and ask, "hey Eric why did you push Kenny?" "I didn't push him, let go of my arm" Eric screamed. The bus driver sits Eric in the front seat for the ride to school. She makes him speak to the assistant principal in the front office, since the other kids also told the bus driver about Eric picking on another kid earlier.

Once the bus arrived at school and the assistant principal Ms. Williams escorted Eric off the bus. They went into her office and sat down across from each other. "Hi Eric, what's going on buddy?" Ms. Williams ask. Tears began rolling down Eric's eyes before he even spoke. Ms. William gives Eric a couple tissues. "Thank you" he said.

"You are welcome sweetheart, is everything okay on the bus? Did anyone upset you? Ms. Williams ask. "No" Eric responded. "Is there anything else you want to tell me? Is anybody else in the school messing with you?" she asks. Eric wiped his face again and said "I'm just a little sad that's all"

"Well" Mrs. Williams said "it's okay to be sad sometimes, that is one of our emotions but you have to be able to handle things like a big boy and do not hurt your friends when you are sad or say mean things, you have to control your emotions"

"Eric you can control emotions by writing things down, talking to a friend or family member, you can pray if you believe in God. Maybe play a video game or read your favorite book. These are just a few of the things that can prevent you from taking your anger out on others." the assistant principal calmly explained.

Eric looked up at her and agreed "I think you are right Ms. Williams, I will practice writing in my journal when I feel sad about things from now on." "Now that is the Eric I know" she smiled, "and if you ever need to talk about what has you so sad, feel free to talk to me or the student counselor Mrs. Jenkins." Eric shook his head okay and left the office.

He left Ms. Williams office and walked to class. He thought to himself how this divorce was making him so mad that he was hurting other people and that is not right. He also knew that even though his parents were divorced he was loved by both his parents. His dad would now be living in another home but that would always be his dad.

Before he went into his class his phone vibrated and he noticed he had a missed text, it was his dad texting him. He opened the message, and his dad wrote he loved him and would be picking him up from school to continue their Taco Tuesday date at Moe's Tacos. Eric smiled so big and walked into class, wow so I am not the problem, he thought.

LOOK OUT FOR MORE KIDS BOOKS!!!